More D[...]

Dark Man

The Face In The Dark Mirror
by Peter Lancett
illustrated by Jan Pedroietta

Published by Ransom Publishing Ltd.
51 Southgate Street, Winchester, Hampshire SO23 9EH
www.ransom.co.uk

ISBN 978 184167 411 7

First published in 2005
Reprinted 2007, 2009

Dark Man

The Face
in the
Dark Mirror

by Peter Lancett

illustrated by Jan Pedroietta

Ransom

Chapter One:
The Old Man

The Dark Man had been given a name.

That had been a long time ago.

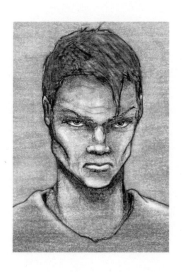

Now he was just the Dark Man.

An Old Man had told him to find the Dark Mirror.

"The Dark Mirror can tell names. True names."

That was what the Old Man had said.

"How will I know the Dark Mirror?" the Dark Man had asked.

"It will be in an evil place. A place of fear."

Chapter Two:
A Place of Fear

So now the Dark Man is here, in a place of fear.

He is under the ground, below an old glass tower.

The glass tower is in the city.

The glass tower is in ruins.

Down here, he must step with care.

There are no lamps down here.

The Old Man had said more.

"Near the Dark Mirror, the walls can bite."

Chapter Three:
The Bite

The Dark Man uses the back of his hand to feel the walls.

It is too dark to see down here.

All at once, the wall feels warm.

All at once, the wall feels damp.

19

The Dark Man pulls his hand away.

There is a sound, like sucking.

The Dark Man's hand is slimy.

It makes him feel sick.

Even so, he must feel the wall once more.

He must find the Dark Mirror.

The Dark Man puts his hand on the wall.

He takes a step.

He feels teeth bite his hand.

Chapter Four:
The Face in the Mirror

The Dark Man feels sick once more.

But at least the Dark Mirror must be near.

Then the wall feels cold.

Then the wall feels smooth, like glass.

It must be the Dark Mirror!

He turns to face the wall.

He cannot see glass.

He can see only black.

Then he sees a face.

A face in the Dark Mirror!

He knows that this is magic, but he is not afraid.

The face he sees is his own.

Then out of the dark he hears a soft word.

"David" it says.

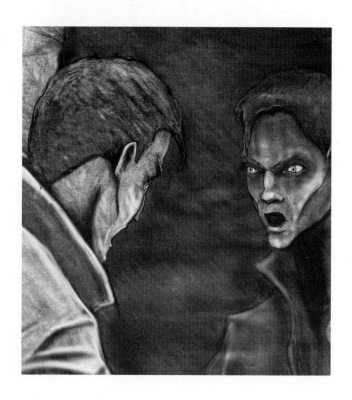

The face in the Dark Mirror says the word again.

"David."

It is the name that the Dark Man once had.

The Dark Man now has his old name.

Yet as he turns to leave, he cannot say why he now feels sad.

The author

photograph: Rachel Ottewill

Peter Lancett used to work in the
movies. Then he worked in the city.
Now he writes horror stories for a living.
"It beats having a proper job," he says.